Percy's Imperfectly Perfect Family

RENÉE C. BAUER

Illustrated by Mark Brayer

Copyright © 2014 Renée Caggiano Bauer.

All rights reserved. No part of this book may be used or reproduced by any means, graphic, electronic, or mechanical, including photocopying, recording, taping or by any information storage retrieval system without the written permission of the publisher except in the case of brief quotations embodied in critical articles and reviews.

Archway Publishing books may be ordered through booksellers or by contacting:

Archway Publishing
1663 Liberty Drive
Bloomington, IN 47403
www.archwaypublishing.com
1-(888)-242-5904

Because of the dynamic nature of the Internet, any web addresses or links contained in this book may have changed since publication and may no longer be valid. The views expressed in this work are solely those of the author and do not necessarily reflect the views of the publisher, and the publisher hereby disclaims any responsibility for them.

Any people depicted in stock imagery provided by Thinkstock are models,
and such images are being used for illustrative purposes only.
Certain stock imagery © Thinkstock.

ISBN: 978-1-4808-1264-2 (sc)
ISBN: 978-1-4808-1265-9 (hc)
ISBN: 978-1-4808-1263-5 (e)

Printed in the United States of America.

Archway Publishing rev. date: 11/24/2014

To Ethan, my creative advisor
...and the rest of the perky bunch,
Kendall, Emerson, and Aiden

Percy was a perky penguin. He listened in school. He did his homework. He was nice to his classmates. He made his nest every morning. Percy had three best friends, Winston the

Walrus, Popper the Polar Bear, and Stella the Seal. They were all classmates in Mrs. Stout's third grade class.

Percy played iceball every Saturday. His dad coached his team and his mom watched all the games. On Sundays, his family would visit Nana and Papa Penguin. His Nana always spoiled him with special treats like his favorite clam bites, sugared icicles and krill ice cream with anchovy sprinkles.

On one particular day, Percy was playing with his shell collection when his mom and dad waddled up next to him and told him something he did not quite understand. They explained that they were going to live in two different igloos. They explained Percy would spend time with each of them in both places. Percy was confused.

. . .

He wasn't feeling very perky the rest of the day.

Later that night, he couldn't sleep. He was sad. He had lots of questions.

• • •

At school the next day, Percy didn't feel like playing with his friends at recess.

"Come on, Percy. Play catch with us," Winston yelled to Percy.

Percy waddled off to be by himself. He didn't want to play. He didn't want to talk to anyone. He wasn't feeling very perky.

After school, Mrs. Stout asked him to stay behind.

"Percy, why the sad face today? You are not your perky penguin self," she asked.

He told her about living in two different igloos.

. . .

"Percy, what does the word family mean to you?" she asked.

He wondered why she was quizzing him.

"Go on, Percy, answer my question."

He thought about what it meant to have a family.

"Family is always having penguins around me who love me no matter what. Sometimes it's my mom and dad. Sometimes it's my cousins or my aunts or uncles," he shared.

She asked, "Do some of those people live in different places?"

Percy giggled trying to imagine all of his cousins living in one igloo. He shook his head.

"Percy, family is not defined by where they live but rather by the love they have for each other."

Percy thought about what Mrs. Stout said that night and he felt a little better. His family is his family, no matter where they all live.

Then he thought, "What if I miss my mom or my dad?" He was sad again.

. . .

The next day at school, he didn't feel like playing with his friends again.

"Come Percy. We are playing hide-n-go-seek," Popper called to him.

Percy didn't feel like playing. He wasn't feeling perky today either.

After school, he stayed behind to talk to Mrs. Stout again.

"Percy, what is bothering you today? I see you are still not your perky penguin self," she asked.

"Mrs. Stout, what if I miss my mom or my dad?"

. . .

"Change is sometimes hard, Percy. It's ok to miss your mom or dad. Remember when you first started Kindergarten how much you missed your parents," she asked?

Percy shook his head up and down.

"What happened after a couple weeks?"

"I started having a lot of fun at school and stopped missing them so much," Percy told her.

Mrs. Stout smiled kindly. Each tooth was the size of Percy.

"Yes, Percy, change is always hard but in time, you will adjust."

Percy thought about what Mrs. Stout said that night and felt better. Then he thought, "Where will all of my favorite things go?" He was sad again.

• • •

The next day at school, Percy was still pouting.

"Percy, we are playing shark in the water. Join us," barked Stella.

Percy didn't feel like playing. He didn't think he would ever be perky again.

• • •

After school, Mrs. Stout waited for him.

"Percy, what is bothering you today? I see you are still not your perky penguin self," she stated.

"Mrs. Stout, what happens to all of my things? I will miss my favorite shell collection if I can't play with it every day."

Mrs. Stout posed the question, "Percy, do you play with all of your favorite things every day?"

Percy responded promptly. "No. Some days I feel like playing with my shells and some days I like to make ice sculptures and some days I like to play games."

Mrs. Stout nodded. "Just like you do different things on different days, when you have two igloos, you will do the same. Certain toys will be at mom's igloo and other toys will be at dad's igloo. You will have favorite things in both homes."

Percy thought about what Mrs. Stout said that night and felt better. Then he thought, "Who do I spend my hatchday with?" He was sad again.

• • •

At school the next day, Percy was still not feeling very perky.

"Percy, come play Capture the Clam with us," Winston called out.

Percy didn't want to participate.

• • •

After school, Mrs. Stout was waiting for Percy.

"What bothers you, Percy? I see you are still pouting."

"Who do I spend my hatchday with?" he inquired. "I will be sad if I can't celebrate with both my mom and dad."

"Percy, what is it that makes your hatchday so special," Mrs. Stout asked?

Percy pondered the question.

• • •

"I get to have cake and blow out candles. I get presents." Percy perked up when he thought of his favorite iceball bat that was his hatchday gift last year.

Mrs. Stout nodded. "Percy, it isn't the day itself that makes your hatchday so special. It is the people with whom you share that time with. Your day will still be special. You will still celebrate with your mom and dad, even if it's at two different times."

That night Percy felt a little better. He knew that his mom and dad still loved him. He knew that sometimes he would miss them but it was ok. He knew that they were still his family. He knew that he would have his favorite things at both igloos.

• • •

The next morning, Percy perked up. He felt better at school and even played ice games with his friends.

• • •

At lunchtime, Popper approached Percy and asked him why he was so sad this week.

Percy shared what was happening at home with his friends.

And his friends started sharing with him. He learned some of his classmates have two homes as well. Almost every classmate knew someone who shared two homes. He felt better.

Percy knew he had some new things to look forward to. Percy loves his mom and he loves his dad.

His family hasn't changed. His dad still coaches iceball and his mom still cheers him on.

Percy still gets treats at Nana and Papa Penguin's igloo on Sundays.

And on his hatchday, Percy got to celebrate twice with two ice cream cakes!

He learned that change does not have to be scary. He learned to share his feelings with his mom, dad and friends and that always makes him feel better.

• • •

Soon Percy liked his two igloos. He liked the special time he got to spend with his mom and dad. He liked having two homes with favorite things at both places.

Mrs. Stout was right. Sometimes change is hard but he soon adjusted.

Percy realized that his family was perfect just the way it was.

• • •

And Percy was a perky penguin again.

Renée Bauer is an experienced family law attorney and mediator. She also represents children in divorce and custody cases. This topic has touched her life professionally and personally. She lives in Connecticut with her son, Ethan, and dog, Sparky.